Five Tales *from*

SHAKESPEARE

written and illustrated by

MEG HARRIS WILLIAMS

CLUNIE PRESS

The author and illustrator:
Meg Harris Williams studied English at the Universities of
Cambridge and Oxford and art at the Accademia di Belle Arti in Florence.
She is an artist and author of several books of
literary criticism, and has taught Shakespeare to primary
school children by means of the stories and pictures in this
book. She lives near Farnham, Surrey, with her husband and
four children.

Acknowledgements:
The author would like to thank Joie Macaulay for literary and
editorial help, Donald Meltzer for advice on the
psychoanalytic perspective of these stories, and the staff and
children of Heatherside Junior School, Fleet, for their
enthusiasm and participation.

First published in 1996 by Clunie Press, Strathtay, Perthshire

Reprinted 1997

Copies of this book are obtainable from your usual supplier or from:
Clunie Press
The Bourne
Redlands Lane
Crondall
Farnham
Surrey GU10 5RF

Tel: 01252 851238
Fax: 01252 850352

© Meg Harris Williams 1996

ISBN 0 902965 30 1

A catalogue record for this book is available from the British Library.

Printed in Great Britain by B.A.S. Printers Limited

CONTENTS

Introduction
WILLIAM SHAKESPEARE

William Shakespeare was born in 1564 at Stratford upon Avon in Warwickshire. He spent most of his life in London where he wrote more than thirty plays and acted in his own company, The King's Men. Some of the parts in his plays were written for particular actors in the company. There were fewer players than parts so the actors 'doubled' as different characters. The plays were performed with little scenery and in everyday Elizabethan dress.

The plays of Shakespeare are written mainly in a type of poetry known as 'blank verse', though the characters also speak in ordinary prose, especially the comic and 'low' characters. This makes the language very rich, able to express a great variety of feelings.

The shape of the plays is very artistic too. Usually each play has a main story and a second story called a 'subplot'. These start off separately but join together by the end. The different events, like the different characters, all have an important part to play in the final picture.

The expressiveness of Shakespeare's plays means that people have never stopped finding them fascinating to read and exciting to watch. Four hundred years after he lived Shakespeare is still our most popular playwright.

A MIDSUMMER NIGHT'S DREAM

Outside the ancient city of Athens there was a wood, where the citizens used to go even as children to play games, explore nature, and welcome the new seasons. Athens was known for its orderly, law-abiding people; it was, after all, sacred to Athena the goddess of wisdom. But the wood was a strange wild place. Here, the law of Athens did not count, even though the wood was so close to the city that you could be there in a twinkling of an eye. It was said to be a favourite haunt of those mysterious immortal beings, the fairies. They would often meet in its shadowy glades to dance and hold their revels. The fairies were invisible to mortal eyes, but they kept a close watch on the lives of ordinary men and women.

At the time of our story, the Duke of Athens was Theseus, a wise and thoughtful ruler. He was about to be married, and the city was planning festivities to celebrate this happy occasion. But suddenly something happened which threatened to spoil it. An Athenian girl, named Hermia, had refused to marry the man her father had chosen for her; she wanted to marry another man because, she said, she loved him and he loved her. The law of Athens, however, said she must obey her father; it could not be changed, however unreasonable it seemed. And it did seem unreasonable, because the man Hermia's father chose had been in love with another girl until a very short time ago, and now he said he had changed his mind. But this girl, who happened to be Hermia's best friend, Helena, was still in love with him. So the four young people found themselves in a mess. They were trapped by the laws of Athens and by their own feelings, and they wanted a way out.

'The course of true love never did run smooth', said one of them gloomily. He was soon to discover how true his words were, not just for himself but for everybody in this story.

As the Duke, Theseus said the law had to be obeyed. But he was unhappy about it, especially as he could see his Queen was upset too. This would be a blight on their own marriage. Inwardly in his heart he hoped there might be some other solution, so he gave the young lovers some time to think about it. Maybe he even guessed that they would decide to run away from Athens that very night, and go to the wood which was outside the reach of the strict Athenian law. Because this is exactly what they did. Hermia told Helena about their plan to elope, and Helena told the man she loved, with the result that all four of them secretly followed one another's footsteps to the wood that midsummer night. All of them were hoping for a solution to love and its problems. And eventually they did find one, but it did not happen at all as they expected.

Now another group of Athenians also stole away from the city that night. They were hoping for some peace and quiet, because they wanted to work on a new and special challenge, quite different from anything they had ever tried before. These were five working men or 'mechanicals', and they meant to rehearse a play of their own, to perform before the Duke on his wedding day. Their names were: Quince, who had written the script and who was a carpenter; Flute, who was a bellows-mender; Snout the tinker; Snug the joiner; Starveling the tailor; and Bottom the weaver. Because it was for a wedding, their play was a story of true love; and they found a good place to practise it, in a sheltered glade beneath an ancient knotted tree known as 'the Duke's oak'.

The story of their play was an old one, well known to all the people of Athens. It was about two runaway lovers, and it ended tragically. The hero kills himself for love because he believes that his lady has been eaten by a lion – although in fact the lion has only taken her scarf. Bottom was the best man among them, so he was chosen to play the hero; and the Lion was to be played by Snug the joiner, with a huge curly mane joined to the top of his scalp, and his own face peering out underneath. Everyone agreed that this was least likely to frighten the real ladies who would be watching the play. As Bottom said,

'A lion among ladies is a most fearful thing.'

If he had been playing the part himself, he would have liked to make a little speech, saying:

'Fair ladies, I would entreat you not to fear, not to tremble. My life for yours: if you think I come hither as a lion, it were pity of my life. No. I am no such thing. I am a man, as other men are.'

In fact, it looked as though Snug was going to be more afraid than any of the ladies; so Quince comforted him by saying that his part was a very easy one, it was 'nothing but roaring'. But Bottom could see that even this roaring was no easy matter. Should the Lion roar loudly, to show his pride and strength, or softly, to show his gentleness in the presence of the ladies? This delicate question had to be taken seriously. Perhaps a mixture of both things could be invented?

'I will roar you as gently as any sucking dove', suggested Bottom helpfully; 'I will roar you as if I were a nightingale'.

Really, Bottom would have liked to act all the parts in the play; he thought they were all wonderful. Quince, who was the producer, had to beg him to stick to one part only – the hero, who was, he said, 'a most lovely, gentleman-like man', so Bottom was the only man among them who could play the lover; and with this Bottom had to be satisfied. However, it was not long before he was given the chance to act a role that was not written down in their script at all. Imagine his friends' astonishment when Bottom disappeared behind a tree for a moment and then came back with an ass's head upon his shoulders! Here was a costume far more extraordinary than Flute with his lady's scarf or Snug with his lion's mane. This was a real transformation.

'Bless thee, Bottom! thou art translated', cried Quince, in fear and wonder.

What astonished his friends most of all was Bottom's own calmness. He refused to be upset like them. In fact, he joked about how they were trying to fool him:

'This is to make an ass of me, to frighten me, if they could', he said to himself.

He could not see his face, but he felt himself to be the same man as ever, beneath the skin. So when the other workmen ran back to the city in confusion and dismay, Bottom stayed put, and strolled around the forest glade singing a little song to show that he was not afraid.

What had happened to Bottom? He did not know it, but he had come into contact with the fairies. He had stepped so close to their strange world that he was about to enter it. Close by him, on a flowery bank, the Queen of the Fairies herself was lying asleep. Bottom, standing behind the tree waiting for his next acting cue, had no idea of this. Nor did he see what was happening when the ass's head was placed on him by Puck, an impish follower of the Fairy King.

The King and Queen of the Fairies were called Oberon and Titania, and they had come to the wood that night from the far corners of the earth to celebrate the Duke's wedding. But they did not arrive here together. They came separately, each with their own train of fairy followers. For the fact was that these fairy rulers were in the middle of a bitter quarrel.

'Ill met by moonlight, proud Titania', were Oberon's first words to his Queen when he saw her there.

'Jealous Oberon', she replied coldly.

The cause of their quarrel was a little 'changeling' boy – half fairy, half mortal – whom they each thought should belong to themselves alone. Quarrelling about who should own this child, they found themselves enemies, and lived apart. Now the fairies knew very well that when they quarrelled, the lives and feelings of the mortals they watched over would also be upset. For the fairies played an important part in the rhythms of nature with its seasons and harvests, and also in the loves, joys and sorrows of human beings. Without their help, the corn would not ripen, milk would not churn into butter, marriages would not be blest and children would not be born healthy. When the King and Queen of the fairies were not working together in harmony, these tasks became neglected, causing much trouble and suffering.

So Oberon was angry; and he called his servant Puck to him. Puck was like a small boy, delighting in mischief; but he never meant any real harm, and was always obedient to his master's commands. Oberon now sent him to gather a special flower with a magical juice which would make anyone instantly fall in love with the first living creature that they saw. Then he anointed Titania's eyes with it as she was sleeping on her flowery

bank. He whispered over her:

'What thou seest when thou dost wake,

Do it for thy true love take.'

And while he had the flower, he remembered the problem of a young mortal couple he had noticed in the wood. Oberon had seen an Athenian girl running after a man and complaining about his hard-heartedness. To his mind this man was behaving badly, so he told Puck to find him and anoint his eyes with the juice, which would make him love the girl in return.

'Cupid is a knavish lad

Thus to make poor females mad',

said Puck, secretly thinking this was a huge joke.

The problem was, of course, that there was not one but two young men in the wood that night, and not one girl but two. Oberon did not yet realise this. So he could not justly blame Puck when Puck came across the wrong man lying asleep on the ground (this was Hermia's love), and anointed his eyes with the magic juice. Nor was it Puck's fault when, as chance would have it, the man was woken up by the wrong girl (this was Helena) and immediately fell in love with her. This was the beginning of a bigger mess than ever. Helena thought it was a cruel joke, and Hermia, when she found out, decided everybody was against her. It was not long before the four friends were all quarrelling furiously with each other. The two men wanted to fight, but Puck (who of course was invisible) led them astray. Soon everyone was completely lost in the dark wood, convinced there was nobody they could trust. So in spite of his good intentions, Oberon's efforts to help the mortal lovers led to greater confusion than ever. Since he had not yet managed to sort out his quarrel with his own wife, perhaps this was not so surprising.

Meanwhile, as all this was going on, Titania was lying asleep and invisible. Her eyes with their magical juice were closed; but in her dreams she understood very well the troubles of these mortals who were supposed to be in her care. After the lovers had passed by, along came the workmen, and began to rehearse their play about love in the very heart of the wood, just where she had her hidden bower. Strange as it was, Titania woke up just when Bottom with his ass's head on was walking around singing his song, the other workmen having run back to Athens.

'What angel wakes me from my flowery bed?' she asked, addressing Bottom directly, and declaring that she loved him.

When she said this, although she was a fairy, she became visible to Bottom, though he was a mortal. He was indeed surprised when he saw who was talking to him, but he replied calmly:

'Methinks, mistress, you have little reason for that.' He thought a bit, and added, 'but reason and love don't keep much company together these days. A pity – we should make them friends.'

Titania's eyes were touched with the love-juice, but she also had her own reasons for liking Bottom the weaver. She was the Fairy Queen and she could recognise his fine qualities. He was not an important ruler like Oberon or Theseus, but as often happens in fairy tales, he had a gentleness of character which highborn princes sometimes did not. Titania was pleased to see him taking a kind interest in the little fairies who attended her, who were like her children. He asked them their names and all sorts of questions and encouraged them to show him the things they could do best. So the fairies gathered honey for him, played music and scratched his hairy face. This was quite different from the way that Oberon had proudly said he should be the one who owned the changeling boy. However strange it was to find himself in Titania's court, Bottom showed he could accept his welcome graciously.

Later, Bottom could never quite believe that it was not a dream, as perhaps it was. Dream or not, this was how it came about that Titania the Queen of the Fairies changed her mind about love. Oberon too learned something from this dream and shortly afterwards he became friends again with his wife. The quarrels of the young lovers could be settled at last. By now they had given up trying to work out who was their true friend. There seemed no reason in love. All they wanted was to get out of the wood. All alone they wandered, not knowing which direction to take, scratched by thorns and briars, exhausted and miserable. Eventually, unable to stumble any further, each one lay down alone to sleep and wait for the next day's dawn. Little did they know that even then, the fairies whom they could not see were carefully guiding their footsteps, and it was Puck who at Oberon's command placed them in their dark beds on the cold ground, and adjusted the juice on their eyes. When they awoke the next morning they found themselves, as if by a miracle, to be two happy couples placed side by side. Hermia was next to the man who had loved her first of all, and who now loved her again; and so was Helena. Nobody could remember how this had happened; the events of the night seemed misty and cloudy, like a dream. But at last they all knew who they really loved, and who loved them in return, and this time they were matched in perfect harmony.

And now everybody could go back to Athens to take part in the wedding celebrations at the palace. The old law of Athens did not matter any more. A new moon was shining in the sky. Bottom's loyal friends were hoping patiently for his return from the wood, and when he did come back they were overjoyed, because now their play could go before Duke Theseus.

'The short and long is', said Quince excitedly, 'our play is preferred!'

The Duke had indeed chosen their play for his wedding, and they were sure that he would be pleased with it, because they wanted to make him happy. Of course none of the workmen had been highly educated like the lords and ladies of the Athenian court. They often got their words mixed up and made many other mistakes which the audience found hilariously funny. The strange thing was, that their mixed-up words and actions really spoke to the newly married lovers in a way which nothing else could have done. Nothing - except, perhaps, some cloudy dream like that of the night before. After all, who could have been more mixed up than the lovers themselves, in the middle of the dark wood? But it took the wise Duke Theseus to guess that there was more meaning hidden here than met the eye.

'Even the best actors are only shadows', he said, 'and the worst are no worse than shadows, if imagination is added to them.'

He saw that some things could only be understood properly if people used their imagination to see them in the right light.

Even so it was hard work, for both the actors and the audience. For all of them, this kind of play was something completely new. When Starveling came on to the stage pretending to be the Man in the Moon, carrying a lantern, dog and thornbush to show who he was, the courtiers thought they would die of laughter. Poor Starveling was beginning to crumple with embarrassment. He forgot his part and tried desperately to explain himself:

'All that I have to say', he said, 'is to tell you that the lantern is the moon, I the man in the moon, this thornbush my thornbush, and this dog my dog.'

They laughed at Starveling because he was supposed to be inside the lantern, not outside it, otherwise how could he be the Man in the Moon? Even Theseus laughed. He was a powerful ruler and he found it difficult to imagine himself in the position of someone like Starveling. Then the Lion rushed in and roared and seized the heroine's scarf. Now the Queen began to understand Starveling's feelings better. She clapped her hands and called out with special kindness:

'Well shone, Moon! Truly the Moon shines with a good grace.'

Hearing this, Theseus knew she was right. So he congratulated the Lion's performance in the same way:

'Well moused, Lion!' he called.

It was the meaning that counted, not just its shadow in the actors. Together with his new wife, he showed he could learn from their childlike and loving spirit. The royal couple set an example for the others, so that in the end they could all be blessed by the fairies.

At midnight, when the play was over, Theseus called for the lamps to be put out, and invited the fairies to step over the threshold of his darkened house.

'Lovers, to bed', he said: ''tis almost fairy time.'

The play ends with the fairies carrying tiny lights into every corner of the palace, making it a holy place, and showing us how the shadowy wood of dreams exists here inside us, even when we cannot see it. The fairies bless the three couples and their children who are not yet born. Then Puck comes forward to say farewell. To encourage us to let our own imagination work, he offers to take our hands and be friends:

> 'If we shadows have offended,
> Think but this, and all is mended,
> That you have but slumber'd here
> While these visions did appear,
> And this weak and idle theme
> No more yielding than a dream ...
> Give me your hands, if we be friends,
> And Robin shall restore amends.'

MACBETH

Many hundreds of years ago, Scotland was a troubled and violent country, split by bloody quarrels between its lords or 'thanes' as they were called. Many thanes wished to bring up their families in security, and enjoy the arts of peace and civilization; but this was difficult when at a moment's notice they might be called to war. Sometimes they judged their own claim to the throne to be stronger or more reasonable than the king's, and they might rise to fight against him; or they might fight on his side against some other enemy. It was as though Scotland were possessed by wicked and destructive spirits which lurked in the darkest corners of the rugged hilly countryside, ever ready to put evil thoughts into anyone at all confused or unhappy.

This is what happened to one of Scotland's brave and noble lords during the reign of King Duncan: he was Macbeth, Thane of Glamis. Macbeth was returning homewards one day after a fierce battle in which he had defeated the treacherous Thane of Cawdor and his allies, and restored power to the King. King Duncan, a white-haired old man, was a good and virtuous king; but he was not a soldier, and could never have held on to his throne without the aid of Macbeth. And Macbeth himself, though fearless in battle, was softhearted at home; his wife said he was filled with 'the milk of human kindness'. As he wended his way across the lonely heath that day after the battle, accompanied only by a trusted friend and fellow-soldier named Banquo, he was troubled by thoughts of home. He was exhausted by the day's fighting, and excited by his triumph; but it was not a healthy excitement - more like being drunk or drugged. Night had not yet fallen, but the sky was dark and foggy, as though it were still filled with the dirty smoke of battle.

When the two weary soldiers reached the most lonely point of their homeward trek, the darkness seemed to thicken and twist into sinister ugly shapes. These were fumes rising from a huge steaming black cauldron; and round it crouched three figures, stirring a mess of horrible ingredients and croaking a hoarse chant:

'Double double toil and trouble

Fire burn and cauldron bubble –'

In the gloomy light of their cauldron they seemed monstrous to Macbeth and Banquo, like aged women with beards and deformed faces. They were, of course, the witches: the evil spirits of Scotland who liked to wreck not only men's bodies but also their minds. Just as they chopped up pieces of human beings and animals and mixed them with dirt and poison for the purpose of their wicked spells, so would they destroy people's minds with poisonous lies. Their words had a double meaning, so that even if they appeared to be full of promise, yet anyone who heeded them would in fact be led to his doom. As Macbeth and Banquo stood there, the witches suddenly looked up and stared at Macbeth; they were expecting him. He was their chosen victim, and they hailed him by his title:

'Hail to thee, Macbeth Thane of Glamis!'

From this, Macbeth saw that they knew who he was. But then they continued to hail him, with further titles which did not belong to him. First they cried,

'Hail to thee, Macbeth Thane of Cawdor!' which was the name of the traitor he had just defeated; and then again they said, most deliberately:

'Hail to thee Macbeth, who shalt be King hereafter!'

And now Macbeth saw that they knew not only his outward face, but also his hidden ambitions, and the borrowed titles which he might have secretly liked to try on and wear. Before he met the witches, he had felt he might have liked to become king some day, if he was given the chance; now, he felt he *had* to become king. It was small wonder he said to Banquo:

'So fair and foul a day I have not seen'.

The witches vanished into thin air; but their prophecy lurked in his mind, like a fatal disease waiting for its chance to erupt and destroy him from within. Though strong in battle, Macbeth could be weak in other ways.

Now his friend Banquo had also been promised success in life by the witches. They told him that one day he would be the father of kings; and like any other lord, Banquo would have been proud to see his descendants rise to a position greater than his own. But he was suspicious of fair promises coming from the mouths of creatures who looked like servants of the devil; and he decided to do nothing, just wait and see. Macbeth, too, would rather have left everything to chance: he said to himself,

'If Chance will have me king, then chance may crown me.'

And at first, it almost seemed as though this is what might happen. For King Duncan was so grateful to Macbeth for saving his kingdom that he told him he owed him everything he had, and he immediately made him the new Thane of Cawdor. It seemed as though the King himself were encouraging Macbeth to believe the witches. Macbeth almost believed that, if Duncan had not had two sons of his own, he might actually have offered him his golden crown there and then. However, he did not. 'Chance' was not going to crown Macbeth by itself.

But as the witches well knew, there was another reason Macbeth could not sit quiet and leave everything to chance. This was his wife. He never tried to hide anything from Lady Macbeth. He told her about his success in battle and about the strange meeting with the witches which had seemed to result in the King's special favour. He also told her the King would be arriving at their home in person that night, to celebrate with them. Now when she heard this, Lady Macbeth was fired with ambition. She immediately decided that Duncan must be murdered in his sleep while he was their guest at the castle. Macbeth had known in his heart that she would suggest this; all the same, he was horrified when she actually said it, and he saw that she meant it. At first he said he could not do it:

'I may do all that may become a man;
Who dares do more, is none.'

He felt with horror that pity was being thrown to the winds, and he could do nothing about it; pity was

'like a new-born babe,
Striding the blast.'

Lady Macbeth told him angrily that a real man would not be afraid to seize what his ambition wanted. Was he a soldier, and afraid? Nothing could be easier than killing someone in their sleep. Moreover, she said – and this is what finally silenced Macbeth – she knew a lot more about pity and innocent babes than he did, since she was a woman; yet she would not shrink from killing even one of these, if it were necessary. Macbeth was defeated by this cruel idea; he could find no answer to this witch-like taunt. He knew he could not resist his wife's ambition. To satisfy her, he agreed to wield the deadly daggers as he had done in the fury of battle; except that this time the killing would take place not on the battleground but in the heart of his home life.

Lady Macbeth was beautiful and welcoming that evening when King Duncan arrived with his two sons. The King praised the food, the hospitality, and the pleasant sheltered situation of the Macbeths' castle, which provided safe nesting-places for the birds. But later that night, the castle was changed into a chamber of horror, closing its battlements and portcullis in a deathly trap like the gates of hell itself. Macbeth believed he could see a dagger in mid-air, leading him onwards to Duncan's room to commit the murder. He whispered in terror, 'Is this a dagger that I see before me?' as he was drawn onwards, following the dagger. It was as if his hands did the murder of their own accord, without his will. In fact he forgot to replace the bloody daggers in the bedroom where they had to be left, and he dared not go back. Lady Macbeth had to do this with her own white hands, and now she felt that she too had truly taken part in the evil deed with actions, not words alone. She was soiled by blood, and later it would come to haunt her, with terrible visions which would drive her mad.

So Macbeth and his wife became the King and Queen of Scotland; but it was as though they had each murdered a part of their own souls. The blood could be washed from the daggers, but however much they washed their hands, in their mind's eye it seemed to pour without stopping. And now Macbeth realised that ambition had cost him the loss of that 'eternal jewel', his soul – worth more than any number of expensive jewels in a king's crown. And in his heart he blamed it on his wife.

The murder of Duncan was only the beginning of the downward course of the once noble Lord Macbeth. He found he could not stop the flow of destruction, and he waded deeper and deeper into bloody deeds. Full of guilt, he became suspicious of everyone he thought must know about it, and ordered their deaths. He suddenly remembered that Banquo had been hailed as father to a line of kings, and that he himself was childless and had no heirs. It made him see the witches' promise in a new light:

'Upon my head they placed a fruitless crown,

And put a barren sceptre in my gripe.'

He had a crown, but nothing to give it a real future, or make it meaningful. There was no point in a crown without heirs. Nobody could trust him or depend on him. Nothing new could come into his life. 'To be thus is nothing', he said; and though he saw now that there was nothing he could do about that, there was one thing he could do – he could kill Banquo and his son. Then at least his heirs would not have a future either. So Macbeth ordered this murder to be carried out in secret, while at the same time pretending that Banquo was meant to be the guest of honour at an important banquet.

'Let us drink', said Macbeth,

'To our dear friend Banquo, whom we miss;

Would he were here!'

Banquo himself would never go to any more banquets – he was dead; but his ghost came instead – at least in the eyes of Macbeth. Sweating with terror, Macbeth cried out, because he was sure he could see the ghost of Banquo sitting on the chair which should have been his. The guests of course could see nothing. But the ghost was so real to Macbeth that it prevented him from sitting down himself: there was Banquo with his head hacked and bleeding in twenty places – a ghost as solid as the witches themselves with their poisonous brew.

But though Banquo indeed was killed, his son had in fact escaped and fled the country, as had Duncan's sons, waiting for their chance of revenge. Next on the hit-list was another friend of Macbeth's – Macduff the Thane of Fife. Macduff was a man of decency and kind heart, like Macbeth before he became enslaved by the witches; and he groaned to see Scotland under the yoke of the tyrant that Macbeth had become. Naturally he was a leader of those who were beginning to want to rebel against him. Now Macduff had a wife, and also children. This time it was not the children who escaped. Macduff had fled to England to seek help from the English king; but in doing so, he had left his family unguarded, and they were all killed in his place, by Macbeth's hired murderers.

Now Macbeth had truly become a murderer of infants. But the more the blood flowed at his hands, the less could he feel of pity or remorse in his heart. He could no longer consider what was right or wrong; gradually he no longer knew the meaning of either joy or suffering. His mind seemed shut away, no longer a part of him; instead he just gave orders for murderous actions as quickly as possible so that he did not have to think too deeply about what it all meant. 'Be it thought and done', he said.

Again he visited the witches, seeking them out in their cavern on the heath, crouched over their steaming cauldron and ready as before to spur him onwards. By now he was possessed by their lies. The witches made him believe that if he knew the future, with their help he could control everything that happened to him. Indeed if he knew the future he was safe, and nobody could ever touch him. So when Macbeth put himself in the hands of the witches, he cut himself off from all human friends, even his wife who had once seemed so close. He needed nobody and nobody needed him. Gradually, though, it pressed on him that there was no real future for such as he: tomorrow, and the next day, and the next, would always bring the same empty, joyless existence:

'Tomorrow, and tomorrow, and tomorrow,

Creeps in this petty pace from day to day,

To the last syllable of recorded time.'

He might be 'safe' from all painful feelings, but there seemed less and less point in being alive at all. And what of Lady Macbeth? Like her husband, she too was shut in a prison of her own making. After the murder of King Duncan, she no longer had any control over Macbeth; he listened only to the witches. Eventually, after hearing how Lady Macduff and her children had been killed, she became mad, and wandered at night about the castle, walking in her sleep. She always had a candle with her as she was afraid of the dark, and could be heard muttering:

'The Thane of Fife had a wife; where is she now?'

The vision of the murdered Duncan as she had seen him that night haunted her in horrid detail; who would have thought the old man had so much blood in him? she asked herself. Still she believed she could never wash the blood off her hands. 'Out, damned spot!' she cried, rubbing them: 'Will these hands never be clean?'

Yet before the murder, Lady Macbeth had been sure that she had complete control over her own mind, and that her husband only had doubts because he was too kind-hearted. Now she was suffering from hallucinations as he had been, and a doctor was called to try to help her. But the doctor said it was not his job to try to heal minds, only bodies.

'Canst thou not minister to a mind diseased?' Macbeth asked him helplessly; he was thinking of his own mind's illness as much as of his wife's. But the doctor replied that only the patient himself could do that.

By now both Macbeth and his wife felt they had lived long enough, and were waiting for fate to bring an end to lives which had become lonely and meaningless. So when the news was brought that Lady Macbeth had killed herself, Macbeth was sad that he could not even truly grieve for her. Ever since becoming king, he had lived in terror of the revenge which he knew he deserved. Yet when this finally came, it was a relief,

since at the same time he was freed from the spell of the witches. The witches had promised him that he could be killed by no man who was born of a woman; and that his reign was safe until the trees of Birnam Wood should walk across the valley to his fortress at Dunsinane. Both these things seemed impossible, so Macbeth believed his position must be fixed and immovable, 'safe' as he despairingly called it. He knew that all his enemies had united with Macduff and were even now gathering against him, but he could feel nothing, not even fear. The witches, he thought, had said that nobody could attack him successfully. He was doomed to be king for ever.

Suddenly the news was brought to him that Birnam wood was indeed marching to Dunsinane castle. This was because the opposing army was advancing against Macbeth under cover of branches broken from the trees, and it looked as though the wood itself was on the march. Macbeth's imagination was awoken, as he saw there was no longer safety for him in the witches' prophecies. For the first time in a long while he felt afraid, but he roused himself and determined to meet his fate bravely. There followed a fierce battle, in which Macbeth came face to face with Macduff, and they fought hand to hand. At first it looked as though Macbeth would win, for he was still the strongest fighter in all Scotland. He said though that he did not want any more of the Macduffs' blood on his conscience. Then Macduff told him a strange thing: that he had not been born in the normal way from his mother, but had been cut from her womb by the hand of a surgeon. When Macbeth heard this, he recognised that here was the man who would be able to kill him.

At last his mind began to clear, melting away the filthy fog of the witches' lies. He no longer wanted the type of false safety they offered, and they had no more prophecies to threaten him with. Macbeth knew now that the righteous fury of Macduff's revenge would inspire Macduff to certain victory in their fight. And only death itself could cancel out the witches' curse on his own life, which had made it a kind of living death, a walking shadow, 'a tale' (he said)

'Told by an idiot, full of sound and fury,
Signifying nothing.'

So though the soldier in him made him fight to the end, Macbeth met his match in Macduff; and Scotland was freed, for a time at least, from the witches' rule.

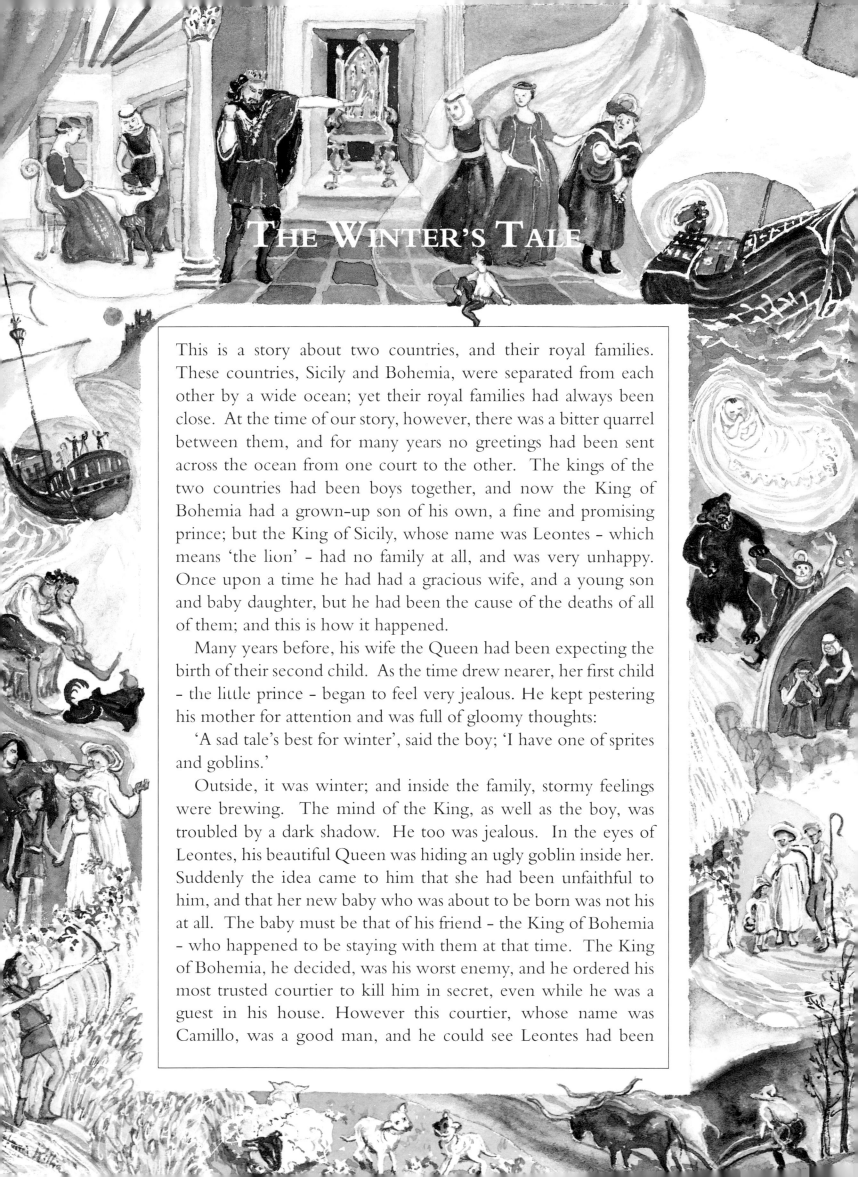

THE WINTER'S TALE

This is a story about two countries, and their royal families. These countries, Sicily and Bohemia, were separated from each other by a wide ocean; yet their royal families had always been close. At the time of our story, however, there was a bitter quarrel between them, and for many years no greetings had been sent across the ocean from one court to the other. The kings of the two countries had been boys together, and now the King of Bohemia had a grown-up son of his own, a fine and promising prince; but the King of Sicily, whose name was Leontes - which means 'the lion' - had no family at all, and was very unhappy. Once upon a time he had had a gracious wife, and a young son and baby daughter, but he had been the cause of the deaths of all of them; and this is how it happened.

Many years before, his wife the Queen had been expecting the birth of their second child. As the time drew nearer, her first child - the little prince - began to feel very jealous. He kept pestering his mother for attention and was full of gloomy thoughts:

'A sad tale's best for winter', said the boy; 'I have one of sprites and goblins.'

Outside, it was winter; and inside the family, stormy feelings were brewing. The mind of the King, as well as the boy, was troubled by a dark shadow. He too was jealous. In the eyes of Leontes, his beautiful Queen was hiding an ugly goblin inside her. Suddenly the idea came to him that she had been unfaithful to him, and that her new baby who was about to be born was not his at all. The baby must be that of his friend - the King of Bohemia - who happened to be staying with them at that time. The King of Bohemia, he decided, was his worst enemy, and he ordered his most trusted courtier to kill him in secret, even while he was a guest in his house. However this courtier, whose name was Camillo, was a good man, and he could see Leontes had been turned into a type of madman by his jealous fury. So instead, he helped the King of Bohemia to flee the country, and they left together. Meanwhile Leontes put the Queen in prison, saying that she would soon be put on trial and punished.

It was in prison that shortly afterwards the new baby was born, a girl. Meanwhile Leontes shut himself in his palace, brooding gloomily, and listening to no-one's advice. There was one person in particular he said must be kept away from him. This was Paulina, a spirited lady who had known Leontes since he was a child. She had no patience with his (or anyone else's) tyrannical rages and tantrums. Paulina was the only person who was not afraid of telling him the truth about himself. The truth, she believed, was the only thing that would 'do him good', and she insisted on getting in to speak to him.

'Let her not come about me', growled the King; 'I knew she would', he added under his breath.

Secretly, everyone in Leontes' court hoped that this lady would be able to influence the King and bring him to his senses. Her idea was to bring the new baby before him, with the Queen's permission; she hoped that the sight of it would soften his heart. So Paulina laid the baby down on the floor in front of everyone. But Leontes hated it – the infant was not his, he thought, so why should he take care of it? He commanded Paulina's husband to take it away and leave it to the mercy of chance in some wild and remote place far from Sicily. Sorrowfully, this old nobleman obeyed. He believed the infant was doomed, unless it was nursed by wild animals – wolves or bears – as had sometimes happened in old tales.

In this way, the cast-out daughter of the King of Sicily came to be left on the coast of Bohemia, the country of the other King. For this is where the Sicilian ship came to land, one dark and threatening day when a violent storm was brewing on the horizon. The old nobleman named the baby Perdita, which means 'the lost one'; for this is what the Queen in a dream had told him to do. Sadly he laid Perdita down on the earth. Then he tried to get back to his ship. But before he could do so, he met one of those wild animals he had prayed might nurse the baby. It was a bear; and it chased him, caught him, and ate him up. At the same time, the ship itself was swallowed by the raging sea and sank. But Perdita remained, safely wrapped in her bundle on the ground.

Meanwhile back in Sicily, Leontes was beginning to suffer the consequences of his jealous rage. So far, nobody had managed to make him change his mind about his wife. He was determined she must stand trial, and he had sent messengers to the oracle of Apollo at Delphi, which he was sure would prove to everybody that the Queen was guilty. But when the verdict of the oracle was read out in front of everyone at her trial, it said that the Queen was innocent, and that Leontes was a jealous tyrant. Hearing this, the court and people rejoiced. Now, at last, Leontes must come to his senses. But to their horror, the King announced,

'There is no truth at all in the oracle.'

At that very moment, the news was brought in that his young son had died from grief because of his mother's trial. Leontes was shattered; he felt he had been struck by a thunderbolt from heaven. The oracle said that he would live without an heir, 'if that which was lost were not found'. He had already lost the baby girl, whom he did not want, and now he had lost the boy too - the hope of his life. Perhaps, said Leontes, he had made a mistake. Hurriedly he promised to try to make the other things right again :- he would send messengers to Bohemia, apologising to the King, and would ask his wife to forgive him. But there was more sorrow in store for Leontes. Paulina came in to tell him that the Queen too had died from grief.

This is how it came about that Leontes, who was once a happy and successful king, had no family at all; and it was all the fault of his own jealousy. Now it was truly winter in his soul. Once he had been too proud to listen to good advice; but now, he begged Paulina to tell him again the truth about his folly, envy and ingratitude:

'Go on, go on' - he said - 'thou canst not speak too much.'

Her sharp but truthful words were the only thing which helped him to remember how much he had loved the wife and son he had lost. He vowed to spend the rest of his life thinking about them, and asked Paulina to help him. Humbly he promised her:

'Once a day I'll visit
The chapel where they lie, and tears shed there
Shall be my recreation.'

Leontes sorrowed for sixteen years. It was like a long, long dream from which he could not imagine ever waking up. And all that time, it seemed as though it were winter in Sicily. Everybody suffered because the King was unhappy and had no heirs. Yet without knowing it, his mind was growing stronger and wiser, just as in winter, many animals and plants are quietly gathering their strength for the return of spring.

And what had been happening in distant Bohemia, the country of the other king? There, without Leontes knowing anything about it, his lost daughter Perdita was in fact growing up strong, wise and beautiful, in the family of a good shepherd who had found her as a baby and adopted her. We remember how the old nobleman had left her on the ground, before he himself was eaten by a bear and his ship was sunk by the storm. Now as it happened, an old shepherd was searching that part of the coast, together with his son, looking for some strayed sheep. When he discovered the abandoned baby wrapped in a bundle on the ground, he took pity on it and decided to give it a home. Then his son came up and told him about the wreck of the ship and the death of the old gentleman, which he had seen with his own eyes.

'You met with things dying', mused the old shepherd; 'I met with things new-born' - and he showed him the baby.

Then they discovered that alongside the baby in the bundle was a bag of gold, more than they could have earned in a lifetime.

'This is fairy gold', said the shepherd. He and his son went home well pleased with the day's discoveries. ''Tis a lucky day', he said, 'and we'll do good deeds on it.'

The time came when Perdita reached the age of sixteen; and she was the queen of the countryside. It was not surprising that the King's son had discovered her while he

was out hunting one day and fallen in love with her. Privately they agreed to marry as soon as it was possible, but they both knew this would not be easy to arrange, since they came from such different ranks in life. So for the time being, not to alarm the old shepherd her father, the prince visited Perdita's home dressed as a shepherd. He knew his own father, the King, had a hot temper and would be furious if he married a simple country girl, so he kept his courtship a close secret from him. However, the King had more idea than his son realised of what he was up to. One day the King decided to go and see for himself the pretty shepherdess whose fame had spread far and wide. He took with him Camillo, the trusted courtier from Leontes' court who had helped him escape from Sicily sixteen years before, and who had since become his own best friend. Then the two men disguised themselves in big cloaks with hoods so they should not be recognised.

The day they chose was the midsummer sheep-shearing feast. This was one of the main country festivals of the year. All the country people, young and old, had gathered under the summer sun to eat, dance and make merry. Perdita was the hostess of the feast. In her festive clothes, garlanded with flowers, she looked - said the prince - like Flora the goddess of spring. The two strangers wrapped in big cloaks thought so too, as she welcomed them and gave them flowers - lavender, mint, savory, marjoram and marigolds. These were flowers of middle summer for men of middle age, she said. To the young people in their spring of life like herself, she would have liked to give spring flowers: violets, lilies, primroses, and especially, she said,

> 'daffodils,
> That come before the swallow dares, and take
> The winds of March with beauty.'

As everyone knew, these were the flowers which Proserpina had lost when, in the ancient legend, she was carried off below the earth to marry the lord of the underworld, in the country of the dead. Every winter she had to stay underground, but every summer she came back and there was sunshine and harvest.

Now the country fairs were haunted by a clown - a vain rogue who went around selling ribbons, knick-knacks and other colourful bits and pieces. Apart from picking pockets when he saw the chance, he was a harmless fool who valued nothing so much as fancy clothes. When he came along, everybody crowded round him wanting to buy presents - except the prince and Perdita. Why didn't he buy a present for his girlfriend? the disguised King asked his son.

'Old sir', said the prince with a patronising air, 'she prizes not such trifles as these.'

As he said this, he seemed to notice a gleam of understanding in the older man's eyes, shining beneath the folds of his hood. Clearly, thought the prince, this man had once been in love himself. Suddenly the idea came to him to have this shadowy stranger witness his official engagement to Perdita there and then. Even now, he still did not recognise that this was his father. The King asked him if he had a father?

'I have', replied the prince, 'but what about him?'

He tried to dismiss the idea of his father, because he knew his father should have been present on this important occasion, and the old shepherd thought so too. Meanwhile the King was getting more and more enraged. At last he could hold in his anger no longer, and he burst out in majestic wrath, stripping off his disguise and saying that he was no old stranger but the King himself! In a flood of rage he threatened to have everybody tortured and executed on the spot. Then he swept away, leaving his old friend Camillo behind to sort matters out with the rebels.

'O my heart!' wailed the old shepherd to his daughter: 'You knew this was the prince!' Now, he said, they were all ruined. But Perdita said she had not been very afraid of the King's anger after all. In fact she had wanted to tell this proud man that the same sun shone on their humble cottage as shone on his court. Then the prince said he was ready to give up his crown for Perdita:

'I am heir only to my affection', he announced.

And when the good Camillo heard how things now stood between these two, he came up with a plan to help them, and which would help him too. For he had been wanting for some time to see his old country of Sicily again, especially as he had heard of Leontes' repentance. Now he suggested that they all went there together, saying that Perdita was the newly wed princess of Bohemia, and that they had come to bring friendly greetings after these many years of silence. So once again, but in the opposite direction, the wide ocean between Bohemia and Sicily was crossed by people who were being driven away by a king's anger. This time, the ship was full. In it were Camillo, the prince, Perdita and all her adopted family – the old shepherd and his son. Even the rogue from the fair managed to get on board (after swopping clothes with the prince). And they all set sail together for Sicily.

In this way Perdita returned to the country of her birth. There she found Leontes, now a much humbler man, still deeply mourning the wife he had rejected those many years ago. His friends begged him to 'forgive himself' for the wrong he had done her, and to take another wife. But he said:

'I cannot forgive the wrong I did myself.'

Then, almost like a dream, the prince and Perdita appeared before him. They told him they came to heal the split between Sicily and Bohemia. Leontes rose from his seat in wonder. He seemed to see the son and daughter he might have had, but had lost, newly created in the fulness of time. A strange feeling of hope stirred within his heart, that for so long had been closed in wintry gloom. He held out his hands to them and cried:

'Welcome, as is the spring to the earth!'

Nor did it matter that shortly afterwards the angry King of Bohemia appeared on the scene, after chasing his son's ship across the ocean. For by now, Leontes had learned to judge better. Thinking of his lost wife and of what she would have wished, he promised to help the young couple by speaking to the prince's father. As it turned out, this was not necessary, because the old shepherd produced the riches which had been in the bundle with Perdita as a baby; these included the scarf and jewel which had belonged to the Queen her mother, and which proved that she was indeed the lost princess.

At last the oracle was fulfilled and Leontes' lost daughter was found. The joy and wonder which now broke out in Leontes' court was so great that it would be impossible to describe it. Everything that had happened seemed as incredible as an old tale. The old shepherd and his son, who were most to thank for all this, were not forgotten but were welcomed into the new royal family. They felt pleased and proud that they were now 'gentlemen born', as they called it. The shepherd's son said excitedly:

'I was a gentleman born before my father; for the king's son took me by the hand, and called me brother; and then the two kings called my father brother; and then the prince, my brother, and the princess, my sister, called my father father; and so we wept; and those were the first gentleman-like tears that ever we shed.'

The shepherd and his son really were gentlemen at heart. So they let the foolish pickpocket from the fair stay with them, though they knew what a rogue he was. And he was happy, because at last he could wear a gentleman's clothes.

But what happened next was stranger than any old tale. Paulina now explained that ever since the death of the Queen, she had arranged for a statue of her to be worked on. Only now, all these years later, was it finished and ready to be seen. So everybody went together to see this wonderful work of art. But before Paulina drew the curtain from in front of it, she warned them to be prepared to marvel, as the stone was so life-like. Even so, when the statue was unveiled, Leontes was awe-struck. He was sure he could see breath stirring between its lips. Next, Paulina called for music, and said to everyone looking on:

'It is required that you awake your faith.'

Then she prayed the statue to come down and 'be stone no more'; at last the Queen could be redeemed from death.

And as they all stood there gazing at the statue, their faith was awoken, and the statue began slowly to move down from its pedestal. It appeared that the stone really was the living flesh of the Queen, returned from the country of the dead. As they watched, the Queen held out her hand to Leontes, and explained that she had held on to her life, though frozen and hidden away, in the hope that Perdita had survived and would one day be returned to her.

At last the moment had come. Life flowed again inside her, and Paulina could say to the newly restored Queen:

'Turn, good lady,
Our Perdita is found.'

The lost one was found, and the King and Queen could turn and embrace one other with a warmth which looked as though it had been lost for ever. Sunshine and joy had crossed the ocean from distant Bohemia, to free the court of Sicily from its deathly spell; and the story of Leontes and his family was no longer a winter's tale.

KING LEAR

There was once a king in Britain named Lear, who had three daughters; his favourite was the youngest, and she was called Cordelia, which means 'drink of the heart'. Lear had a long and happy reign. Eventually, however, he felt the time had come to give up the cares of government. His daughters and their husbands could take over all that. But he was so used to having everyone under his command that he could not imagine not being king himself. He expected that if he divided up his kingdom amongst his daughters in a very clever way, he would still be powerful and important. So he decided to call all the members of his court together, and then in front of everybody, to ask each of his daughters in turn how much they loved him.

Now his family and friends privately thought this was a very foolish way of carrying on. They suspected it would prove nothing except that Lear was a person who, in spite of his age, did not know much about either the world or himself. He was old but not wise. His elder daughters however were keen to have power in the kingdom, and they decided to humour their father. So they made fine and fancy speeches about how extraordinarily much they loved him. These flattering words satisfied the old man, and he gave them each one third of his kingdom. Then he turned to Cordelia, expecting her to make an even finer speech, so he could give her the richest part of his kingdom. But Cordelia loved him dearly, and she thought it was time he learned to face the truth, instead of acting in vain shows with her hypocritical sisters. So she said she loved him as her father, neither more nor less, and that she had nothing more to add.

Cordelia's answer, of course, entirely spoiled Lear's performance. He had wanted everyone to see that he was loved more than anybody had ever been loved before, and that Cordelia was the jewel in his crown. He had always had a hot temper, and now his rage began to boil up inside him. An old friend of his named Kent, his counsellor, saw what was coming and tried to calm him down. But Lear could not control his feelings:

'Do not come between the Dragon and his wrath', he growled.

In a fury, he banished both his counsellor and his daughter. Cordelia went to marry the King of France; while Kent left the court, wondering in his heart if he could still help his old master, perhaps secretly in disguise.

'See better, Lear', were his parting words.

Now the kingdom was entirely in the hands of Lear's elder daughters, and he was dependent on them for everything. These daughters saw their father as a foolish old man - noisy, obstinate and a troublemaker. They thought he was likely to become a great nuisance unless he and his friends were kept in their place. So instead of being indulgent to him in his old age, they decided to act together, and cut him down to size. At first, when he was in their houses, Lear was allowed a hundred knights of his own; but soon it was only fifty, then none at all. Now he had no house or courtiers of his own. The only follower who clung to him faithfully and could by no means be sent away, was his Fool.

Every king had a Fool of his own - the only person in his entire court who could be relied on to tell him the truth, however unpleasant it might be. Other people might flatter the king to serve their own turn, but not the Fool. Because of this, the Fool was often looked on as being a little bit mad, as having a 'little tiny wit'. It was not long before Lear's daughters shut their father out of their homes altogether - and when this happened he turned to his Fool, the only person who seemed truly to belong to him.

'O Fool!' he said; 'I shall go mad.'

While he spoke these words he heard the thunder of an approaching storm. Since they were not allowed in the palace, Lear and the Fool stumbled out on to the barren, windswept heath. There they were joined by Kent, who had indeed found a way to help support his old master, disguising himself as a poor servant. The storm promised to be a wild and terrible one - no night for anyone to be out on the heath. Kent had found a small hovel or shack nearby, and he began to lead the old King in that direction for shelter. As he moved slowly towards it, Lear wondered what he had done to deserve his sufferings:

'I am a man more sinned against than sinning', he told his friend.

He could not understand how he had sinned, but he was beginning to understand some other feelings which he had never known before. When he had lived in comfort and luxury, he had never given a thought to the many poor people in his kingdom who had known pain, cold and hunger. For them, every day was a struggle to get even the bare necessities of life. As he told the Fool,

'The art of our necessities is strange'.

Then Lear was angry with his old kingly self, as he had been in the days when he had more than he needed, and never thought to share it with others:

'Expose thyself to feel what wretches feel' (he told himself),

'That thou mayst shake the superflux to them,
And show the Heavens more just.'

He thought the heavens which were shaking the tempest over his head could also shake life's blessings more fairly over all the people.

Gradually Lear was coming to realise how wrong he had been in believing all his life that being loved would mean he never had to suffer. Perhaps everybody suffered, but he had never known it. In this way they came to the hovel which his friend had found. The Fool went in first; but then he ran out, crying aloud in alarm as though he had seen a monster. For the hovel already had somebody in it – and now he appeared!

Out sprang a young man dressed like a beggar in nothing but a few rags, daubed with dirt and shivering with cold.

'Tom's a-cold', he said when he saw them. Then he started to babble nonsense like a madman. The Fool was frightened; but Lear immediately took a liking to this man, and decided to stick close to him. In fact he called him his 'philosopher'. This was because the more he listened to him and asked him questions, the more he found he could learn from him – lessons which an entire lifetime as King had not managed to teach him. This mad philosopher, who called himself Poor Tom, was naked; so Lear decided he too would throw off his clothes. His clothes were just 'lendings'– not part of his real self, and hiding the true nature of the man underneath. Truth was bare and simple, not 'sophisticated' like fancy clothes. The real thing, Lear decided, was like mad Tom, the 'unaccommodated man':

'Unaccommodated man is no more than such a poor, bare, forked creature as thou art. Off, off, you lendings!'

As he said this Lear pulled off his rich clothes, because he felt they were just like the flattering words of the court: they did not mean anything, in fact they were lies, like those his elder daughters had told him, and he did not want to be flattered any more. He wanted to know who he really was, when all the pomp that surrounded a king was taken away.

Now as it happened, Tom was not the real name of this young man, nor was he really a mad beggar. He was Edgar, the son of the Earl of Gloucester, who was an old man like Lear himself. Gloucester had been very unhappy about what was happening to Lear and his kingdom. He had wanted to help him, but was not quite brave enough to defy Lear's elder daughters, who were after all the new rulers he was supposed to obey. But Gloucester was also unhappy about what was happening in his own family. In fact he had another son besides Edgar, and he was secretly unsure which of his two sons truly loved him. In the same way, his other son suspected he was not really loved by his father, so he decided to plot against his brother by telling their father lies about him. Then, he thought, he would be the favourite son and heir instead of Edgar. Because of these lies, Edgar had to hide himself away, and this was why he had disguised himself as a mad beggar and fled to the wild heath where nobody would recognise him. But the bad brother was not content with disgracing Edgar. He had tasted ambition, and now he saw a way of becoming the Earl of Gloucester himself, even quicker. So he betrayed his own father to Lear's elder daughters, saying that there was a plot to put the old King back on the throne. Now it seemed there were no limits to the cruelty of those two sisters. They were so angry that they gouged out old Gloucester's eyes. Before, he had been blind to the lies of his bad son; now, he was truly blind.

'Is there any cause in nature that makes these hard hearts?' Lear asked his philosopher, Mad Tom (who was really of course Edgar in disguise). The more Lear tried to find a reason for his daughters' cruelty, the more mad he became himself. He needed Edgar to help him try to understand the meaning of his life and the painful feelings he had to suffer.

But Edgar also had to look after his own father. After he had been blinded and cast out, Gloucester came staggering over the heath, thinking of the old King, because he had seen him there the night before. He thought also of the strange mad beggar whom he had noticed with him at that time. For some reason, this beggar had made him think of his lost son Edgar. Gloucester knew now that he had been wrong to reject him. Although he could no longer see, he felt clearer in his mind, and hoped to make fewer mistakes, such as the mistake he had made about his sons. As he explained, sadly:

'I stumbled when I saw.'

Like Lear, he now knew that he could not escape the painful things in life. He had begun to realise this when the cruel sisters had blinded him, and he had said then:

'They have tied me to the stake and I must stand the course.'

But he wished he might meet Edgar once again before he died, at least to see him in the sense of touching him and speaking to him. Though he did not realise it, even as he said this, Edgar was standing next to him. Edgar felt he could hardly bear to carry on playing his part; but somehow he knew that for his father's good, he must not yet reveal who he really was. They had another journey to make, and more to learn, before this could be done.

By now, Cordelia with her husband, the King of France, had arrived at Dover with an army, to try to avenge the old King. So the cruel sisters were preparing for war. At the same time they were quarrelling with each other because they had both decided that they loved the bad son of the Earl of Gloucester. He was excited by this; perhaps he might even become King. At last, he thought, he knew what it was to be loved!

So the armies from all sides were gathering at Dover. Meanwhile the two old men, Lear and Gloucester, were each making their way towards Dover, separately, for their own reasons. Lear hoped he might meet Cordelia again. But Gloucester wished to be led to the top of one of Dover's high cliffs so he could throw himself over it. He wanted to end his life, since he had lost his son Edgar, who was more precious to him than his eyesight. But even now, Edgar was at his side, acting as his guide. In the middle of a field, they stopped.

'Hark! do you hear the sea?' said Edgar, pretending they were on the very edge of a high cliff. He described the sea stretching out below them into the far distance, and boats and people looking as small as mice. The sight, he said, made him dizzy, and he was afraid of toppling headlong:

'I'll look no more,
Lest my brain turn' he cried.

Gloucester was satisfied: this was the place he wanted. He thanked his guide for bringing him there. Then he threw himself down on the grass, believing he was going over the cliff to a place where painful thoughts and feelings no longer existed. Then Edgar spoke again, this time putting on a countryman's accent to disguise his voice. He told his father he had been thrown over the cliff by a devil, but that he had survived. It was a miraculous escape.

'Bear free and patient thoughts', he advised his father.

Gloucester promised that from then on he would bear his troubles until they ended themselves. He would not seek death before his time. Even though life was difficult, he would be patient. For as Edgar explained to him:

'Men must endure
Their going hence, even as their coming hither:
Ripeness is all.'

It was important to live life to the full, even when death was so near.

Then as father and son were talking together in the field, Lear appeared. He was wandering alone, garlanded in wild flowers which he had picked from amongst the waving corn. Cordelia had sent people out to look for him, but Lear kept escaping from them, believing in his madness that he was being hunted like a dog. Edgar thought it was a heart-breaking sight, and one which he could not have believed if he had not seen it for himself:

'I would not take this from report', he said to himself;
'it is,
And my heart breaks at it.'

Yet he could see now that this was the way things had to be for the old men. It was the only way they could become wise. Edgar listened as they began to speak to each other with a new understanding, and words full of meaning. Gloucester told Lear that although he had no eyes, he could 'see feelingly' - he could see with his feelings. Lear nodded; he could well believe it. Perhaps, thought Edgar as he watched them, there is 'reason in madness'. Behind his father's tragic scarred face, and the old king's wild and crazy looks, perhaps a deeper wisdom was growing. Then, Lear described how he could understand things better now that he seemed to be mad:

'When we are born' (he said) 'we cry that we are come
To this great stage of fools.'

Infants come crying into the world; and it is the same with old men, when they get ready to leave the world. At last Lear had learned to be his own philosopher. Now he could even give advice to Gloucester; and he said exactly what Edgar had also been telling him:

'You must be patient.'

In fact, Gloucester did not have to be patient much longer. The journey of his life was nearly over. This time, he did manage to 'stay the course': he did not try to escape from painful feelings, and at last he was rewarded. For soon after this meeting, Edgar judged that the time was ripe to reveal who he was to his father, and how he had been his companion all this time. When he heard this, the old man's heart burst with a mixture of grief and happiness, and he died. That was the price of finding his son.

Lear's journey too was nearly completed; but before this he had still more of both joy and sorrow coming to him. Cordelia had found him at last; but then she and Lear were captured together by the enemy. Lear did not mind this; he was happy to be in prison with Cordelia. He felt he was safe at last and would never have to be parted from her again:

'We two will sing like birds in a cage', he said.

But he was wrong; this was something which could never be. For Cordelia was murdered in the prison by an order which Gloucester's bad son had sent earlier. He had repented of it, after his brother Edgar had defeated him in a duel; but it was too late – the deed was done. Cordelia was hanged, and Lear could not prevent it, even though – old man as he was – he killed the murderer with his own hands.

The two cruel sisters had also been killed, so now all Lear's daughters were dead. But Lear was filled with a new strength. Carrying Cordelia's body in his arms, he walked into the camp where Edgar and the others, including his old friend Kent, were waiting for him.

'My poor fool is hanged', he said; perhaps he was also remembering his own Fool, who had died on the heath while Cordelia was away. As he laid her heavy body down, Lear knew that she was 'dead as earth' and would never return to him. But at the last minute, gazing at her lips, he also believed that her spirit lived, and that he had found her again. Now at last his own cup of sorrow and of joy was full, as Gloucester's had been. He too was ready to die, though he had been stronger than his friend, and lived longer.

It was left to Edgar to take up the responsibility of the new kingship: he who had helped both the old men with the burden of their sufferings. To everyone who remained on the field of battle, he spoke the last words:

'The weight of this sad time we must obey;
Speak what we feel, not what we ought to say.
The oldest hath borne most: we that are young
Shall never see so much, nor live so long.'

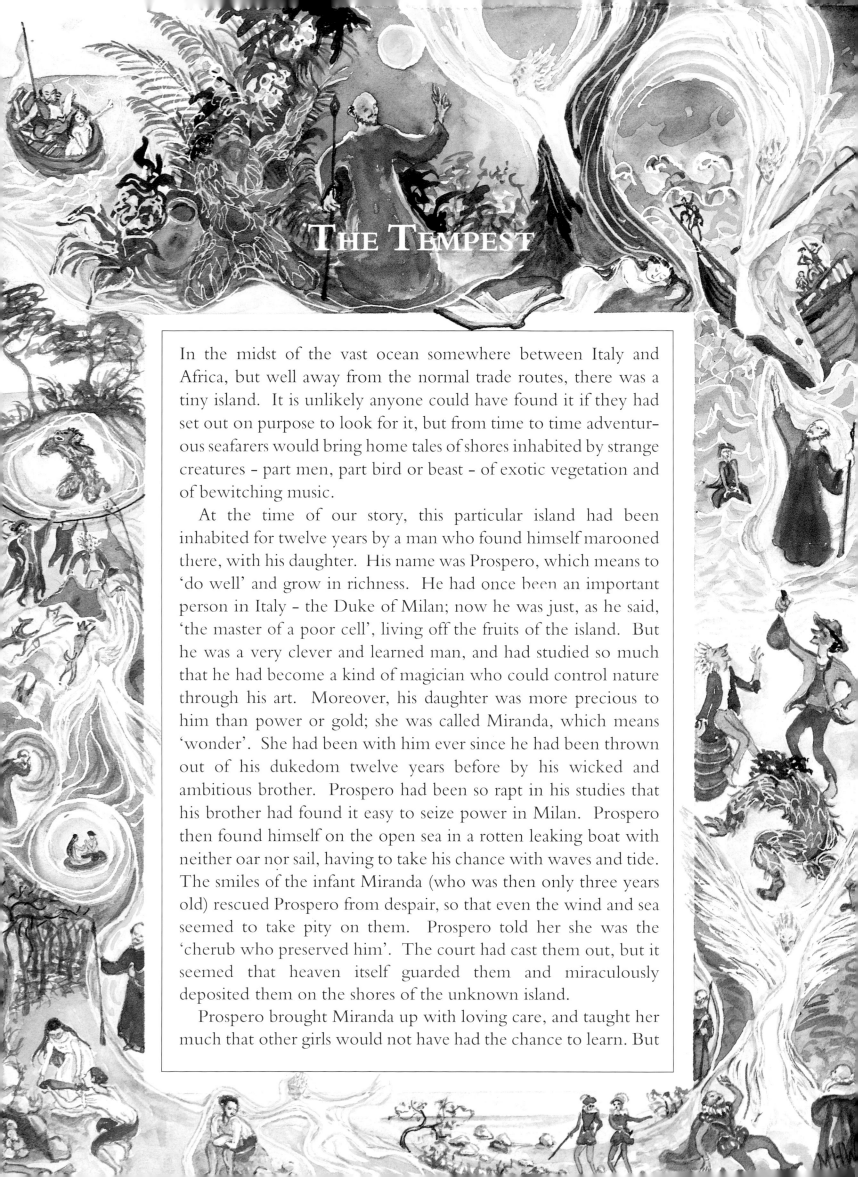

The Tempest

In the midst of the vast ocean somewhere between Italy and Africa, but well away from the normal trade routes, there was a tiny island. It is unlikely anyone could have found it if they had set out on purpose to look for it, but from time to time adventurous seafarers would bring home tales of shores inhabited by strange creatures - part men, part bird or beast - of exotic vegetation and of bewitching music.

At the time of our story, this particular island had been inhabited for twelve years by a man who found himself marooned there, with his daughter. His name was Prospero, which means to 'do well' and grow in richness. He had once been an important person in Italy - the Duke of Milan; now he was just, as he said, 'the master of a poor cell', living off the fruits of the island. But he was a very clever and learned man, and had studied so much that he had become a kind of magician who could control nature through his art. Moreover, his daughter was more precious to him than power or gold; she was called Miranda, which means 'wonder'. She had been with him ever since he had been thrown out of his dukedom twelve years before by his wicked and ambitious brother. Prospero had been so rapt in his studies that his brother had found it easy to seize power in Milan. Prospero then found himself on the open sea in a rotten leaking boat with neither oar nor sail, having to take his chance with waves and tide. The smiles of the infant Miranda (who was then only three years old) rescued Prospero from despair, so that even the wind and sea seemed to take pity on them. Prospero told her she was the 'cherub who preserved him'. The court had cast them out, but it seemed that heaven itself guarded them and miraculously deposited them on the shores of the unknown island.

Prospero brought Miranda up with loving care, and taught her much that other girls would not have had the chance to learn. But now she was of marriageable age and he knew that it was time for her to return to the world of men; yet with all his knowledge and magic he could not have arranged this. They were prisoners on the island. Then, outside his influence, another strange chance occurred like that which had brought them to the island twelve years before. Once again the seas and winds drew a ship to its alien shores. And as it came within the orbit of Prospero's magical powers, it was struck by a raging tempest, split by lightning, and sank to the bottom of the sea.

Or so it appeared, to the eyes of father and daughter as they watched from the shore. But Prospero knew there was more to this sea-storm than met the eye.

'The hour's now come', he said to Miranda.

For the ship was full of his old enemies: the power-hungry brother who had usurped his dukedom, together with the King of Naples who had conspired with him, and also his wicked brother. In fact there was a whole company of courtiers on their way back home to Italy after celebrating the marriage of the King's daughter to an African prince. The King's son (who had been innocent of all the plotting against Prospero) was also on board ship, and so was a good old lord who had tried to help Prospero when he was cast adrift all those years ago, by providing him with books, food and clothing in his leaky boat.

Miranda wept with pity as she heard the cries of the sailors and saw the fine vessel split. She was sure there must have been 'some noble creature' in it, and suspected her father might have caused the storm to rise up in the first place through his artful powers, so she begged him to calm it.

'Tell your piteous heart', he said, 'there's no harm done.'

He promised her that there was no life lost; everyone was safe; even the ship itself was whole and tucked away in harbour, with the sailors asleep under the hatches. And all this was because the time had now come for her to learn more fully who she really was, and where she had been born. Then as Miranda fell into a charmed sleep, the source of Prospero's magical tempest appeared.

This was Ariel, a strange creature who seemed all made of fire and air, and who was visible only to Prospero. Ariel's special quality was 'to fly,

To swim, to dive into the fire, to ride

On the curled clouds ...'

Ariel had been on the island before Prospero arrived, but had been imprisoned in a tree by a witch. He was in pain and misery because it was his very nature to be free, to ride the elements high in the sky, or deep in the earth and below the sea's surface; he could create both roaring storms and healing, soothing music. When Prospero discovered Ariel in the tree he set him free, but on condition he should serve him for twelve years, according to his swift and airy nature. Now the time was nearly up, and Ariel demanded to be altogether free, to fly of his own will not anyone else's. But Prospero could not let Ariel go now; the ship of men had arrived, and this was the most important moment of his life. He needed Ariel's extraordinary qualities for just a few hours more. So desperate was he that he threatened to shut Ariel again in the tree unless he helped him, so Ariel agreed.

Now Prospero had another unusual helper, a native of the island. This was Caliban, and he was the son of that same witch who had imprisoned Ariel and who ruled the island before Prospero arrived. Prospero loved Ariel but he had come to hate Caliban, and now Caliban hated him. Just as Ariel was fiery and spirit-like, so was Caliban earthy, ugly and beast-like. Caliban was strong, and did many necessary tasks for Prospero and his daughter, such as chopping and carrying wood. But he also knew more than anyone else about the nature of the island - which plants were edible, how to catch fish, where to find fresh water. He loved to listen to Ariel's music in the trees, though he had never seen Ariel himself. All these were gifts of the island, and he had shown them to Prospero when he first arrived on the island. At first Prospero had petted him and tried to teach him things - how to use language, how to name the sun and moon. Miranda too taught him what she knew and played with him. But the time came when Miranda was no longer a child but a beautiful young woman. Caliban, ugly beast though he was, was suddenly filled with the desire to possess her. He tried to seize Miranda for himself, but was stopped by Prospero, who was so angry that he imprisoned Caliban in a cave and never let him out except to do his heavy work. Because Caliban no longer had the freedom to roam the island which was his home and element, he hated Prospero and everything he'd taught him, including language:

'You taught me language, and my profit on it is, I know how to curse!' he cried.

Caliban did not dare escape from Prospero's cave on his own, because he knew Prospero would punish him with painful cramps and pinches. Even so, because of Prospero and Miranda, he still admired the cleverness and beauty of mankind, and was eager to share his knowledge of the island. It seemed to him a great stroke of luck when one day he met two of the men who had escaped from the ship during the recent tempest. There were still strange rumblings going on in the sky. These two men, who were a foolish pair, were not sure whether Caliban was a man, a fish or a devil. Caliban thought at first they were spirits sent by Prospero to torment him. One of them had a large bottle of strong wine with him, and when Caliban tasted this extraordinary stuff it completely turned his head.

'That's a brave god', he said to himself, 'and bears celestial liquor. I will kneel to him.'

He decided this fellow with his bottle was near enough a god, and would make a better master than Prospero with his book; so he said to him:

'I'll show thee every fertile inch of the island;

I will kiss thy foot; I prithee, be my god.'

This foolish man, whose name was Stephano, had already drunk a good deal and was filled with self-importance. Since everyone else on the king's ship must have been drowned, he thought, it would be pleasant to be king of this island; instead of being a servant himself, Caliban could be his servant, and every now and again he would give the others a sip of drink to remind them.

'O brave monster!' he said to Caliban: 'lead the way!'

And Caliban sang:
'Ban ban Cacaliban
Has a new master – get a new man!'
But these two fools were not the only ship's passengers to escape drowning. As Ariel assured Prospero, they had all been landed safely on the island, in different groups. Ariel alone knew where they all were, and could fly invisibly and instantly between them, keeping watch. In one corner of the island sat the King of Naples, mourning the loss of his beloved son, who he was sure was drowned. Trying to comfort him was the old white-bearded lord who had long ago helped Prospero. With them were two wicked brothers – the King's and Prospero's. These two, out of boredom, were busy hatching yet another plot: this time to kill the King and seize his throne. (Ariel of course made sure they did not get the chance to carry out their plot.) In the eyes of these conspirators, the island was not full of excitement like the court; it was merely a barren desert. But the others, according to their different natures, viewed the island differently: the good old lord tried to imagine how it could be made into a better society than the one they had at home – how it could become a true commonwealth, where everybody had what they needed; while to the King, the island was nothing but the grave of his son. Nothing could rouse him from his grief.

Nothing, that is, except Ariel. Ariel had been instructed by Prospero to work upon the hearts and minds of these stranded courtiers. So he appeared before them in the shape of a monstrous birdlike creature, huge and terrifying, and held them paralysed as he spoke to them in awesome tones about the crimes of their past life:

'You are three men of sin', he said, 'whom Destiny
        ... the never-surfeited sea
Hath caused to belch up you.'

Only if they were truly sorry for their sins would they ever be able to leave the island. Ariel's speech was majestic and full of grace. Even so, only one of those guilty men was moved by it. This was the king, who remembered his part in the banishment of Prospero, and was convinced that all the powers of nature had gathered to make him suffer, through the death of his son. This must be the cause of the tempest that had sunk his ship.

But what of the prince? On the ship, he had been filled with lightning fire by Ariel, then jumped into the waves and struck out bravely for the shore. There Ariel had left him sitting and thinking sadly. And as he sat there, Ariel sang him a song about the father he had lost:

> 'Full fathom five thy father lies;
>   Of his bones are coral made;
> Those are pearls that were his eyes:
>   Nothing of him that doth fade,
> But doth suffer a sea-change
>   Into something rich and strange.'

As the prince wondered where this strange music was coming from, he saw Miranda. To him, she seemed like a goddess, and he was sure she was the source of the music.

'O you wonder!' he addressed her; and she replied, 'No wonder, sir, but certainly a maid.'

Prospero saw that they had immediately fallen in love, and this fulfilled his highest hopes.

'Spirit, fine spirit!' he whispered to Ariel, invisible beside him. 'I'll free thee within days for this!'

But before the young people could be married, Prospero knew they had some work to do. He needed to put their love to the test to help make it strong and enduring. So he pretended to be angry with the prince, and though he was of noble birth, he made him do Caliban's low work of chopping and carrying logs. The prince discovered he didn't mind doing this, for Miranda's sake. And though Miranda told her father he was harsh, she found the prince looked more noble in her eyes, not less, when he was working hard carrying logs; and then she wanted to carry logs with him. The lovers had passed Prospero's test, and he planned a spectacular wedding celebration for them, using all his art, with lots of spirits in fine costumes, dancers, and music.

At the height of the entertainment, however, Prospero remembered Caliban. Ariel had told him how Caliban with his two foolish drunken companions had been plotting against his life. This did not in itself frighten Prospero, because he knew it would be easy enough to upset their plot. But the sudden thought of Caliban's hatred crossed his mind like a dark and stormy cloud; it made all his efforts seem worthless, and unreal. He knew the newly married lovers didn't need his artful shows any more - that was all 'vanity'; indeed they didn't need him, Prospero, any more, however fond they were of him. Immediately Prospero dismissed the dancing spirits and they 'melted into air, into thin air' like the unreal toys of fancy they were. He explained to the young couple that eventually all life would melt in the same way, like a dream:

'We are such stuff
As dreams are made of; and our little life
Is rounded with a sleep.'

But the last thing on the young people's mind was death. It was real to Prospero, but not to them. Prospero knew they could not understand his trouble, and now more than ever he needed Ariel:

'Come with a thought', he called; 'I thank thee. Ariel, come.'

Together, he and Ariel took hunting dogs and hunted the drunken fools all over the island until the drink was beaten out of them and they came to their senses.

Now in spite of the bottle of wine, Caliban had already begun to find his new master Stephano sadly lacking in judgement. It seemed he could not tell what was really valuable from what was just rubbish. For a start he and his friend were frightened by the strange and wonderful music of the island, which had often given Caliban such rich dreams:

'in dreaming', he explained to them,

'The clouds, I thought, would open, and show riches
Ready to drop upon me: that when I wak'd
I cried to dream again.'

But even after he had explained this, all Stephano cared about was getting his music 'for nothing', without having to pay for it. Caliban could not get him to concentrate on the important business of killing Prospero and seizing his magic book; without this his new master could never be ruler of the island. So Prospero found it easy to trap these foolish conspirators by hanging out a washing line of fine and fancy clothes; as soon as Stephano saw these, he had to stop and dress up like a king.

'Let it alone, you fool', cried Caliban. 'It is just trash.'

Even before the hunting dogs arrived, Caliban had begun to see that he was a fool himself to 'take a drunkard for a god.' He knew better now, and said he would learn to 'seek for grace'.

'At this hour', said Prospero,
'Lie at my mercy all my enemies.'

He promised Ariel that in a few minutes he should be free. But first he must make his peace with the King and his men. Ariel said that he was holding them spellbound outside Prospero's cell: there they stood, the sorrowful King of Naples, the good old white-bearded lord, and the two wicked brothers. Ariel said that if Prospero could see them now, his feelings towards them would soften, and his wish for revenge would melt.

'Mine would, sir, were I human', Ariel added.

Prospero thought about this. If Ariel, who was made of air, could feel sorry for these men, could not he Prospero, a human being, feel sorry too? Would it not be better to forgive his enemies than to punish them?

Prospero knew now that he could no longer rule as a magician over this island of dreams. It was time to throw away his books and to break his magic staff. His 'rough magic' was over. The good people had learnt all they could from him, and the bad people could never learn. Their souls were no longer in his hands. So Ariel woke all the courtiers together from their strange dream, and as they gradually returned to their senses, Prospero revealed himself. To the wondering King he showed his lost son, who was playing a game of chess with Miranda.

'O brave new world!' cried Miranda when she saw all these people. She was the youngest there, but her wonder was echoed by the oldest, the noble lord, who saw that people who had never really known themselves, now had the chance to know themselves a little better:

'In one voyage,' he said,
    'we all of us found ourselves
When no man was his own.'

The good old lord could not know it, but this was as true for Prospero as for everyone else.

'Be free, and fare thou well!'
were Prospero's last words to the spirit he loved; Ariel was free at last. But Caliban, a dark shadow in his life, had come home to him and once again called him 'master'.

'This thing of darkness', said Prospero in front of everyone, 'I acknowledge mine.'

The ship was waiting to take everyone back to Naples – except Caliban who belonged with the island. Would Prospero go with them – back to Milan where, he said, he would be thinking of his grave?

At the end of the play, Prospero comes forward alone and asks us to forgive his faults and pray for him, for at the end of the day, mercy towards men is in the hands of heaven.

'As you from crimes would pardoned be,
Let your indulgence set me free.'